for Martin, Marissa,
Eva and Jonathan
M.B.

for my clever niece Jo
H.C.

ORCHARD BOOKS
96 Leonard Street, London EC2A 4RH
Orchard Books Australia
14 Mars Road, Lane Cove, NSW 2066
ISBN 1 86039 348 9 (hardback)
ISBN 1 86039 663 1 (paperback)
First published in Great Britain in 1997
First paperback publication 1998
Text © Mara Bergman 1997
Illustration © Helen Craig 1997
The right of Mara Bergman to be identified as the author and Helen Craig
as the illustrator of this work have been asserted by them in accordance with
the Copyright, Designs and Patents Act, 1988.
A CIP catalogue record for this book is available
from the British Library.
Printed and bound in Singapore.

BEARS, BEARS EVERYWHERE!

Mara Bergman

illustrated by Helen Craig

 ORCHARD BOOKS

I love bears so much, I do,
and once my dream of bears came true.
I wished and wished and wished for bears,
bears, bears everywhere!

First there was a loud
knock knock
on the door.
The bears skipped in –

ONE

TWO

THREE

four...

a very large bear
with very large paws,

an orangey bear
with long painted claws

and the loveliest bears
I had ever seen –

one wearing blue

and the
other
green.

They went to the kitchen for something to eat
and messed up the floor with their big furry feet.
They climbed on the table and climbed on the chairs,
and then they climbed up the twenty-one stairs…

Ding Dong!
went the bell,
and what a surprise
to see more bears,
of every size!

'Hello, hello! Your wish has come true!
We're here to spend the day with you!"

They padded in
and joined all
the others,
up in my
bedroom and –
OH NO!
– in my mother's.

Big bears, little bears,
round bears
and square,
bears wearing sweaters,
bears that were bare –
bears, bears everywhere!

Up on the ceiling,
spinning
and reeling!
Trying on dresses,
making too
many messes!

Bears on the rugs,
on the lamps
and in boxes,
bears in my drawers
trying on
all my sockses!
BUT...

What was that sound?
What had they found?
A crash, a break…
was my wish a mistake?

A pile of books
and all of my toys
fell –

CRASH! BANG!

on the floor with
more and more noise.

A sad little bear,
dressed all in green,
was stuck underneath –
he could hardly be seen!

We struggled, we sweated, we said, "Oh my!"
We pulled and pushed, had one last try

and he was FREE!

But what were all the others doing?

Tugging, shoving, shouting, booing,
                    running, jumping, hullaballooing...

                              It was then I had to say,

"STOP!
Though I love you so,
Bears, you will have to go."

At first they said, "Oh no, no, no!
You wished for us – we will not go!"
What in the world was I to do?

Suddenly, certainly, I knew.
I wished and wished and wished
for bears to LEAVE!

One by one they slipped away,
all the bears that came to play.

Not a single bear was there.

No bears — anywhere!

It was quiet and still, until…

there was a tiny knock at the door,

and so I opened it

once more...

...to find who I'd been waiting for!